Bunnies on the Go

Bunnies on the Go

Getting from Place to Place

By Rick Walton

Illustrated by Paige Miglio

HARPERCOLLINSPUBLISHERS

Vacation time is here, and so
Pack your bags. It's time to go.
Bunnies, we'll be traveling far,
Every bunny, into the . . .

Car

Bunnies driving through the streets,
Safely belted in their seats,
Up a highway, down a <u>lane</u>.
Now, bunnies, all aboard the . . .

Train

Bunnies hear the clicks and clacks
Of iron wheels on iron tracks.
And see the smoke! Is this a dragon?
Here we are! Climb in the . . .

Wagon

On and on the draft horse walks
While wheels squeak and Grandma talks
Of all the fun they'll have. In fact her
Bunnies get to ride a . . .

Tractor

Bunnies plowing straight and slow,

Up and down the fields they go.

The ride is over much too soon.

Now, bunnies, up in the . . .

Balloon

Bunnies looking from up high
Watch the country passing by.
Through the sky the bunnies float.
Now, bunnies, jump into the . . .

Boat

Across the lake the bunnies glide,

A wet and windy bunny ride.

The shore is here. The anchor strikes.

Now, bunnies, climb onto your . . .

Bikes

Bunnies pedal over the hills,
Chasing, racing, taking spills,
Jumping ditches, getting stuck.
Now, bunnies, hop into the . . .

Truck

Bouncing over the mountain road
With its tired bunny load,
But not too fast, it's dangerous.
Now, every bunny, on the . . .

Bus

Bunnies sing and bunnies yawn,
As the bus rolls on and on.
A good night's sleep is necessary.
But wake up! And board the . . .

Ferry

Across the bay, from shore to shore,
Bunnies watch the seabirds soar.
But, bunnies, now it's time to grab
Your things and jump into the . . .

Cab

Bunnies wave good-bye to places
That they've seen as the taxi races
Down a highway, up a lane.
Now, bunnies, time to board the . . .

Plane

Happy bunnies on the go
Watch the tiny world below.
The bunnies love to ride and roam,
But best of all is coming . . .

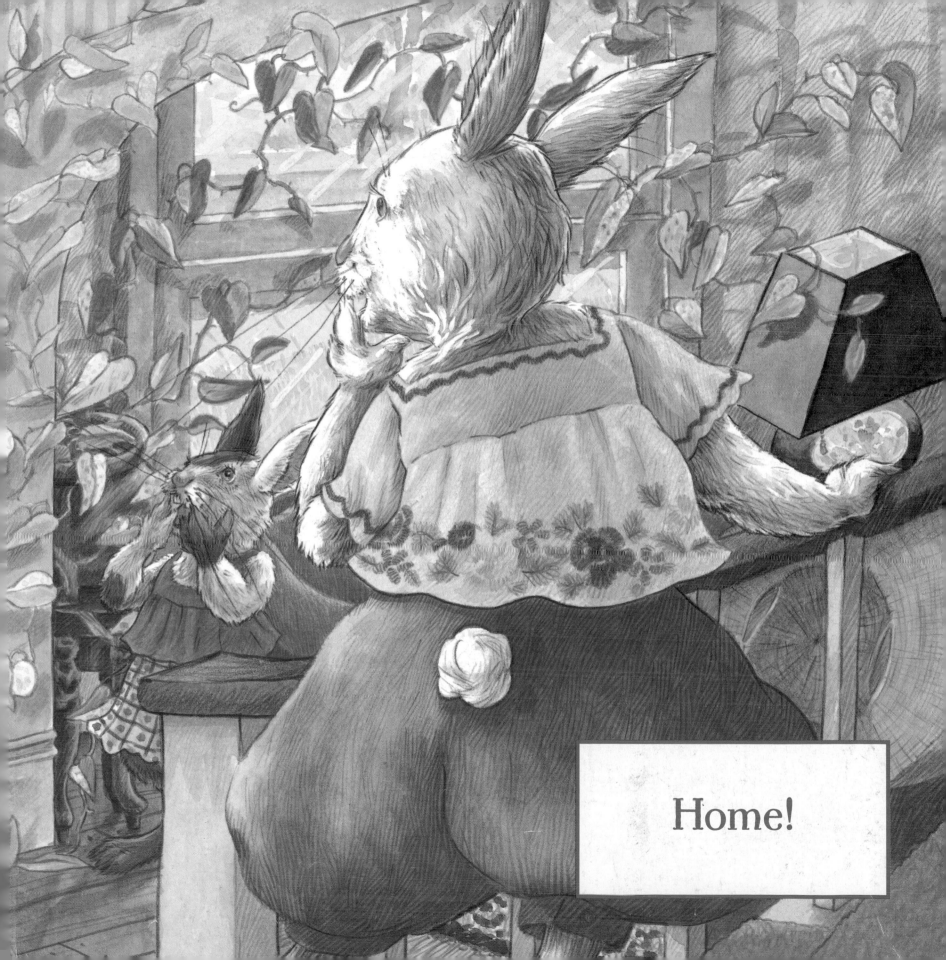

Home!

To Carolee and Terry Ferris,
and their bunnies, who are always on the go
—R.W.

For Marcus and Babeth,
and their bunnies on the go, Nina and Cosmo
—P.M.

Bunnies on the Go: *Getting from Place to Place*
Text copyright © 2003 by Rick Walton   Illustrations copyright © 2003 by Paige Miglio
Printed in the U.S.A. All rights reserved.   www.harperchildrens.com

Library of Congress Cataloging-in-Publication Data   Walton, Rick.
Bunnies on the go: getting from place to place / by Rick Walton ; illustrated by Paige Miglio.— 1st ed.   p.   cm.
Summary: A bunny family takes a trip using many different types of transportation, including car, train, balloon,
ferry, and tractor.   ISBN 0-06-029185-0 — ISBN 0-06-029186-9 (lib. bdg.)
[1. Transportation—Fiction.   2. Rabbits—Fiction.   3. Stories in rhyme.]   I. Miglio, Paige, ill.   II. Title.
PZ8.3.W199   Bs   2003   2002001178   [E]—dc21

Typography by Carla Weise
1 2 3 4 5 6 7 8 9 10
❖
First Edition